Spanish in the World

Dear Reader

The Spanish once led the world. Their explorers sailed further than explorers from other countries. Their soldiers seized more land and grabbed more treasure than any other country's soldiers. The Spanish Empire was once the most powerful empire in the world.

FROM THE 1500s UNTIL THE 1800s, SPAIN WAS THE RICHEST COUNTRY IN THE WORLD.

Today, Spain no longer has the same vast empire. But its influence still exists all around the world. In this book, find out how Spain came to be so important, and why Spanish is one of the most widely spoken languages on Earth.

In this book, you can even find out how to build your own empire!

John Parsons

NELSON
CENGAGE Learning™
For learning solutions, visit **cengage.com.au**

Contents

SPANISH IN THE WORLD

1 Spanish Worldwide

The **Spanish** Language

Today, over 350 million people speak Spanish as their first language. It is one of the most widely spoken languages in the world. Mandarin Chinese, Hindi and English are three others. People speak Spanish in:

- Argentina
- Bolivia
- Chile
- Colombia
- Costa Rica
- Cuba
- Dominican Republic
- Ecuador
- El Salvador
- Equatorial Guinea
- Guatemala
- Honduras
- Mexico
- Nicaragua
- Panama
- Paraguay
- Peru
- Puerto Rico
- Spain
- Uruguay
- Venezuela

Spanish is the first language of some people in other countries, too. These include Belize, Gibraltar, the USA, Andorra and the Philippines.

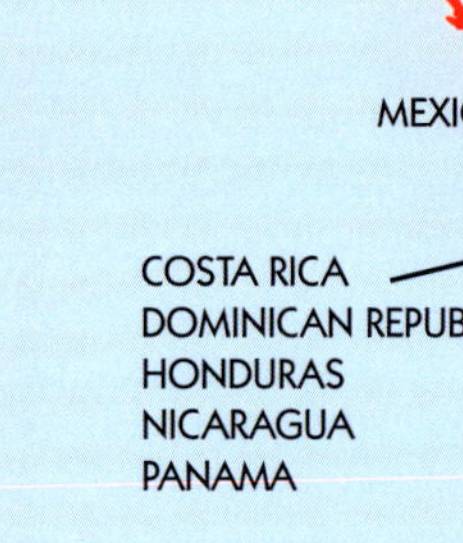

Why Is Spanish Spoken Worldwide?

From the 1500s until the 1800s, Spain was the richest country in the world. It had an enormous empire that stretched around the globe. Everywhere that Spaniards went, people started speaking Spanish!

So what was the secret of the Spaniards' success? Many famous explorers helped to build the Spanish Empire. Find out how!

2 Granada Is Conquered!

From **Granada** to **Spain**

Before 1492, the country that is now Spain was called Granada. It was a mixture of peoples and languages. The Moors, who spoke Arabic, ruled Granada and other areas.

In 1469, King Ferdinand and Queen Isabella were married. Ferdinand ruled the Kingdom of Aragon. Isabella ruled the Kingdom of Castile.

The New Kingdom of Spain

In 1492, Ferdinand and Isabella's armies defeated the Kingdom of Granada. They drove the Moors out.

Ferdinand and Isabella then formed the Kingdom of Spain. Their language became the language of the new country – Spanish.

They also started the Spanish Inquisition. It forced people to become Roman Catholics. If they did not, they had to leave Spain. Many were killed.

The first step in building the Spanish Empire had been taken.

Queen Isabella and King Ferdinand

The Moors in Granada

In the early 700s, almost all of the area known as Spain was conquered by people from North Africa. These people were called Moors. Their new kingdom and its new capital city were both called Granada.

the Alhambra castle, Granada

The Moors valued learning. They helped to spread the learning of the ancient Greeks into Europe. They also invented our number system.

The Kingdom of Granada prospered. Farmers produced more food with new crops and new farming methods.

The Moors left behind beautiful architecture and gardens, such as the Alhambra castle in the city of Granada.

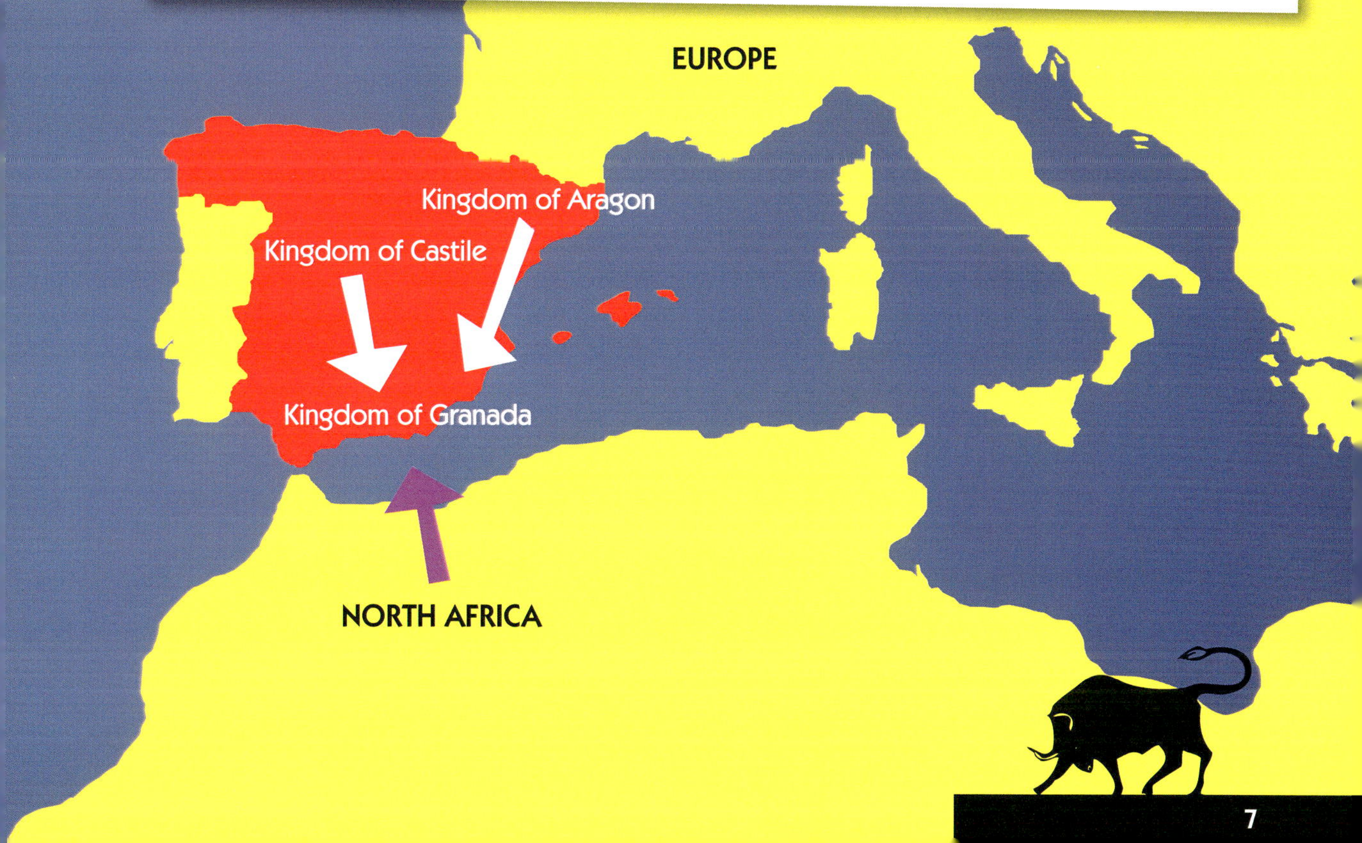

EUROPE

Kingdom of Aragon

Kingdom of Castile

Kingdom of Granada

NORTH AFRICA

A "Recipe" to Build an Empire

Use Your Imagination

Imagine that you want to start an empire like the Spanish Empire. How can you get started?

If you already own a country, here's a simple empire-building recipe to follow. It's worked all over the world and, if you follow the instructions, it's bound to work for you, too. Have fun!

What You Will Need

- A country
- A lot of money
- Some ships
- Some soldiers and plenty of weapons
- Explorers and people with new ideas
- Parts of the world that no one from your culture has travelled to yet.

EXPLORERS

Christopher Columbus (1451–1506) and Ferdinand Magellan (1480–1521) were famous explorers who helped build the Spanish Empire.

Preparation Time

Your first explorations may take between one and three years. You will need a further 10 to 20 years to attack, conquer and settle in any parts of the world you find. However, once started, a good empire can last for over 300 years.

Steps

1. Once you have gathered the ingredients, introduce your explorers to people who have new ideas, and wait until they come up with a plan.
2. Ask your explorers to tell you about the positives and negatives of their plan. For example, the Spanish explorers found a quicker way to India. This meant that the Spanish traders could follow the new trade routes to buy cheaper and fresher spices, which they then brought back to Spain to sell for a lot of money.
3. Combine your explorers with a sprinkling of ships and soldiers, and order them to start exploring right away. The ruler of a neighbouring country might also want to start an empire, so it's good to get there first.
4. Pour your mixture into parts of the world that no one from your culture has explored before.
5. Allow your empire to rise slowly, removing any troublesome people who already live in your new lands.
6. Your empire is ready to enjoy!

Columbus Had a New Idea

In 1492, Spanish explorer Christopher Columbus had an idea to find a new way to the spice markets in India. King Ferdinand and Queen Isabella agreed that it was a good plan, so Columbus set sail the same year.

4 Spanish Explorers Set Sail

Columbus Discovers America

In 1492, Christopher Columbus set sail and discovered America by accident. He made a mistake in his maths. He thought it would be quicker to get to India by travelling west over water, rather than east over land.

If Columbus had done his maths correctly, he would have realised that travelling west made the trip much longer. But then he might not have found the Americas and claimed them for Spain.

MATHS MISTAKE

Travelling east from Spain to India is about 8000 kilometres. Travelling west is about 40 000 kilometres!

NO, LET'S GO WEST, IT'LL BE QUICKER!

LET'S GO EAST TO INDIA!

SPAIN

INDIA

OOPS! WE SHOULD HAVE GONE EAST TO INDIA

"I knew I should have paid more attention in maths class!"

Columbus Goes for Gold

Columbus was sure there were huge amounts of gold in the Americas. So he went back time and time again, trying to find gold. He was not concerned that the gold he was looking for belonged to someone else!

Columbus was made governor of the islands that are now called the West Indies. But he wasn't very good at governing, so the king of Spain fired him in 1500.

The **Spanish** Claim the **Pacific Ocean**

In 1513, the Spanish Empire got a huge boost from a Spaniard called Vasco Núñez de Balboa. His ships crossed Panama in Central America, and claimed the Pacific Ocean and all the lands beside it for Spain. He probably didn't realise what a gigantic ocean he'd just claimed!

Vasco Núñez de Balboa's discovery led the way for Ferdinand Magellan's exploration.

Earth Science

The Pacific Ocean

The Pacific Ocean is the largest ocean on Earth, covering over 155 million square kilometres. There are over 135 000 kilometres of coastline around it. Magellan gave the Pacific Ocean its name, which means "peaceful sea" in Latin.

Vasco Núñez de Balboa discovers the Pacific and claims it for Spain.

ARE WE THERE YET?

Magellan's Explorations

Ferdinand Magellan (1480–1521) was Portuguese. But no one in Portugal wanted to pay for his explorations. So he offered to work for the Spanish, and explored new lands for King Charles of Spain.

Magellan was the first European to discover the Philippines, in 1521. He claimed the Philippines for Spain but he died there in the same year. His ships continued the voyage but only one of the five ships returned to Spain in 1522. Magellan's ship was the first to sail right around the world.

The Spanish Empire was growing!

Life and Physical Sciences

The Magellan Name

Magellan "lends" his name to a South American penguin, called the Magellanic Penguin. Its wings are so rigid, it can "fly" under water.

Two tiny galaxies in space are also named after Magellan. The Magellanic Clouds were discovered in the 1500s, and sailors on Magellan's ships used the clouds to help them navigate during their voyage to the Philippines and around the world.

Ferdinand Magellan

5 Cortés Conquers the Aztecs

Weapons and **Disease**

In 1519, the Spanish decided they needed more lands. They wanted to have all of what is now Mexico as part of their empire. Part of it was home to the Aztec Empire. So Hernán Cortés (1485–1547) was sent to conquer the Aztecs and take their land.

Cortés was a Spanish conquistador who had more powerful weapons than the Aztecs. His vicious dogs and huge horses were trained for war. His men brought diseases that were new to the Aztecs. They had no immunity to measles, smallpox or influenza. The Aztecs tried hard to defend their land, but fighting and illness defeated them. The Aztec empire crumbled and disappeared. It had lasted for almost 500 years before the Spanish arrived.

SMALLPOX

Smallpox is a deadly disease caused by a virus. For many years smallpox was one of the world's most dreaded plagues.

CONQUISTADOR

"Conquistador" is a Spanish word meaning "conqueror". Spanish soldiers were called conquistadors.

a conquistador's helmet

conquistadors marching past an Aztec temple

6 Pizarro Conquers the Incas

Go Ahead Anyway!

The Spanish Empire was getting bigger and bigger. Francisco Pizarro (1475–1541) wanted to lead his conquistadors further south from Panama. The Spanish governor wouldn't allow him to go, but the king of Spain did!

Pizarro Heads South

Pizarro organised Spaniards and Native Americans who also didn't like following rules, and went south. He started a war against another powerful empire, the Incan Empire.

Pizarro and his 168 men were cruel. They had armour, horses and better weapons. They were also fearsome fighters. They conquered the Incan Empire in 1532. Pizarro founded the city of Lima, which is now the capital of Peru.

The Government Palace is in present-day Lima

The Spanish built many churches in Lima.

Today, many people live in poor conditions in some parts of Lima.

Pizarro and his conquistadors defeating the Incas

Social Studies

The Incas

The Incas began as a tribe in Peru. They conquered neighbouring tribes and soon controlled most of Peru and Ecuador. The Incan Empire grew by offering neighbours wealth and power if they joined the empire.

The Incas built magnificent buildings and were skilled in medicine. They made fine fabrics, precious metals and pottery. Unfortunately, the Spanish melted down their gold and silver metalwork for treasure.

the ruins of Machu Picchu, an Incan city

7 Treasures of Gold and Silver

Treasure Ships

The Spanish used South America as a base to find new colonies, like the Phillipines, which Miguel López de Legazpi discovered in 1565. They took land and treasures from the local people. Everywhere, they collected vast amounts of gold, silver and precious stones.

They shipped the treasures home to Spain. Great galleons, full of gold and silver, sailed from the Caribbean to Spain.

Pirates Attack the Spanish

Unfortunately for the Spanish, pirates in the area got rich by attacking their galleons and stealing the treasures.

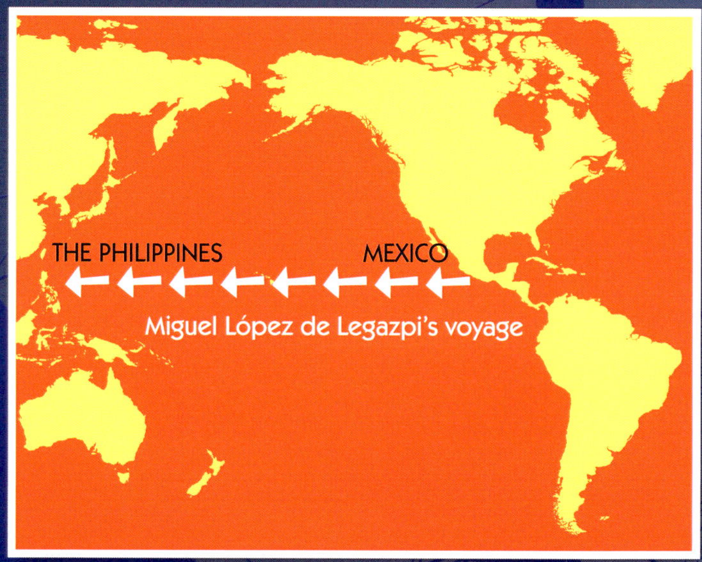

In 1565, Miguel López de Legazpi sailed from Mexico to the Philippines. He started a Spanish colony there as well.

A galleon sails into the sunset.

Pirates capture a Spanish galleon.

Social Studies

Eternal Gold

The Spanish melted down priceless art treasures in gold. Gold from the Incas and Aztecs is still worn today all around the world. Gold doesn't rust or wear out, so it can last forever – unlike empires!

gold dust and gold bars

8 Finding Treasures to Eat

Spicy Treasures

In 1506 Ferdinand Magellan discovered the Spice Islands in the East Indies (now known as Indonesia). Spices were very valuable so that discovery made a lot of money for the Spanish Empire. As well as spices, ceramics and silk were shipped between the Philippines, Mexico and Spain.

More Edible Treasures

The Spanish discovered other edible treasures from the New World, such as chocolate. They also discovered potatoes and corn, and brought them back to Europe. Other things that found space on board the gold-laden galleons were chillies and tomatoes.

SPICES

Spices have been used for thousands of years to flavour food. Some valuable spices shipped to Europe included cinnamon, nutmeg, cloves and mace.

Social Studies and Economics

Spanish Put Prices Up

Even the Spaniards who never left Spain wanted to be rich. They put their prices up so things like bread and salt became very expensive. When people have more money, higher prices can be charged for things such as food or clothes. As prices go up, people need even more money. When they get more money, prices go even higher. This cycle is called "inflation".

All the foods on this page originated in South America (clockwise from top left: potatoes, chillies, corn, chocolate and tomatoes).

9 End of a Vast Spanish Empire

Emigration and Invasion

Many Spaniards moved to South America in search of a better life. Over 250 000 moved during the 1500s and over 500 000 moved in the 1600s. The problem with empires, as the Spanish soon found out, is that the people you conquer are not happy about it.

By the 1800s, almost every country in Europe had decided it was going to have an empire. The French, under Napoleon, invaded Spain in 1808. Suddenly, the Spanish had to defend their own country.

Independence from Spain

In Ecuador, people had had enough. In 1809, while the Spaniards were busy fighting at home, the local people declared independence. The idea of self-government spread across Central and South America. Soon, many countries were declaring independence from Spain.

The Richest Empire Ends

By the start of the 20th century, Spain had lost all of its territories in North, Central and South America. The Spanish no longer had the richest and biggest empire in the world.

Spain Today

Spain is still an important country in Europe and around the world. Because of Spain's empire building activity, there are people all over the world today who speak Spanish. They enjoy Spanish styles of food, and beautiful Spanish architecture exists in many cities. Spanish songs, music and art have influenced people in many countries. For better or worse, Spain has certainly left its mark on the world.

a Spanish statue and architecture in Mexico

a church in the Balearic Islands, Spain

crowds enjoy the night-time lights in Barcelona, Spain

Index

Glossary

emigration	The movement of people from their home country to another, usually permanently
galleons	Large wooden sailing ships, usually used for carrying people and goods
governor	Someone who rules a country or state on behalf of somebody else (such as a king)
immunity	Natural resistance
independence	Having the right to govern, make rules and pass laws without having to ask another country or ruler
plagues	Diseases that cause illness and suffering among large numbers of the population
self-government	Government that is run by people from the country being governed, not by a foreign country
Spanish Inquisition	A period in Spain where religious freedom was severely restricted